First English-language edition published in 2019 by Enchanted Lion Books,
67 West Street, Studio 317a, Brooklyn, NY 11222
Originally published in French by Albin Michel Jeunesse as *Gisèle de Verre*
Copyright © 2002, 2019
Translated from French by Claudia Zoe Bedrick
Final Layout and hand lettering (US edition): Sarah Klinger
All rights reserved under International and Pan-American Copyright Conventions
A CIP record is on file with the Library of Congress
ISBN 978-1-59270-303-6
Printed in China by Toppan

First Printing

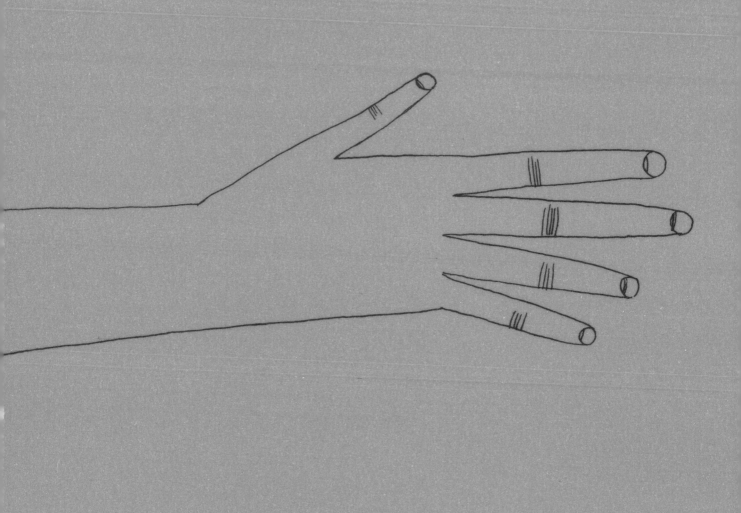

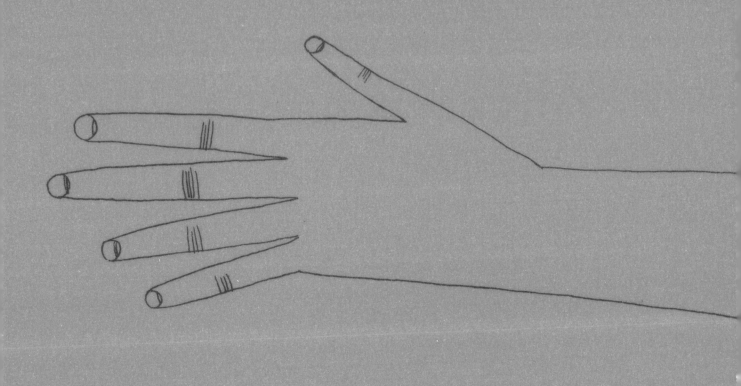

Beatrice Alemagna

Child of Glass

Translated from French by
Claudia Zoe Bedrick

ENCHANTED LION BOOKS
NEW YORK

*O*ne day, in a village near the cities of Florence and Bilbao, a child of glass was born. A girl, called Gisele.

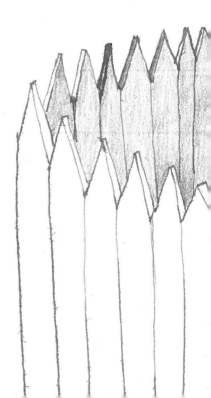

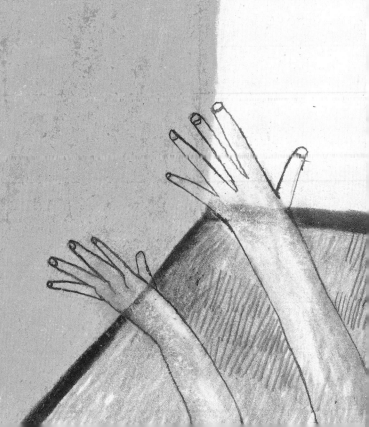

She had large, lovely eyes, delicate fingers, and something so clear and luminous about her... but she was also completely transparent.

Gisele shone and sparkled,
blending with everything around her,
changing color when the sun set
and shimmering like a thousand
mirrors beneath the moon.

$\mathcal{P}$eople came from far and wide to see her.

"Simply incredible!"
"What beauty!"
"Can we touch her?"
"Does she talk?"
"Can we patent her?"
"But how do you find her
in a crowd?"
"Have you thought about
insuring her?"

*B*ut none of that meant anything to Gisele or her parents. What worried them was something else entirely.

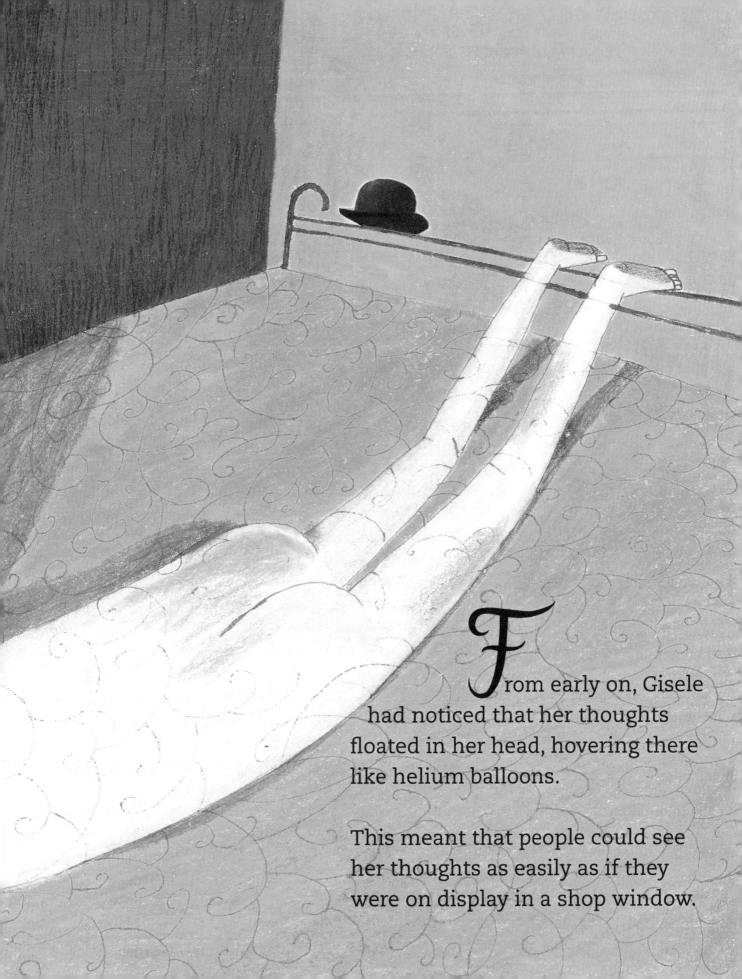

From early on, Gisele had noticed that her thoughts floated in her head, hovering there like helium balloons.

This meant that people could see her thoughts as easily as if they were on display in a shop window.

All one had to do to see her worries was to look directly at her head. And so, whenever she showed the smallest fear or doubt, she would be reassured, without ever having to say a word. In this way, she was easily understood throughout her childhood.

*B*ut as Gisele grew, she realized that her life was far from easy. Behind her transparent forehead, beautiful thoughts as well as awful ones revealed themselves. It was impossible for her to hide her feelings from others.

*H*ighly sensitive as she was, as soon as she felt sadness or anger, one of her nails or one of her legs would develop a tiny crack.

images

1000f
à la livraison

facilités de paiement
jusqu'à 12 mois
conformément à la législation en vigueur

Et en complément nous vo
offrons

1 Grande
couverture
laine garantie
taille 200 x 240

port, ENVOYEZ CE BON PAR RETOU

People grew cross with her. "Can't you keep your thoughts to yourself?" they would say.
Or, "Aren't you ashamed to show such awful things, Gisele?"

Finally, Gisele decided
it was too much.

Sparkling and luminous, sensitive and transparent, Gisele packed her suitcase, kissed her parents and left.

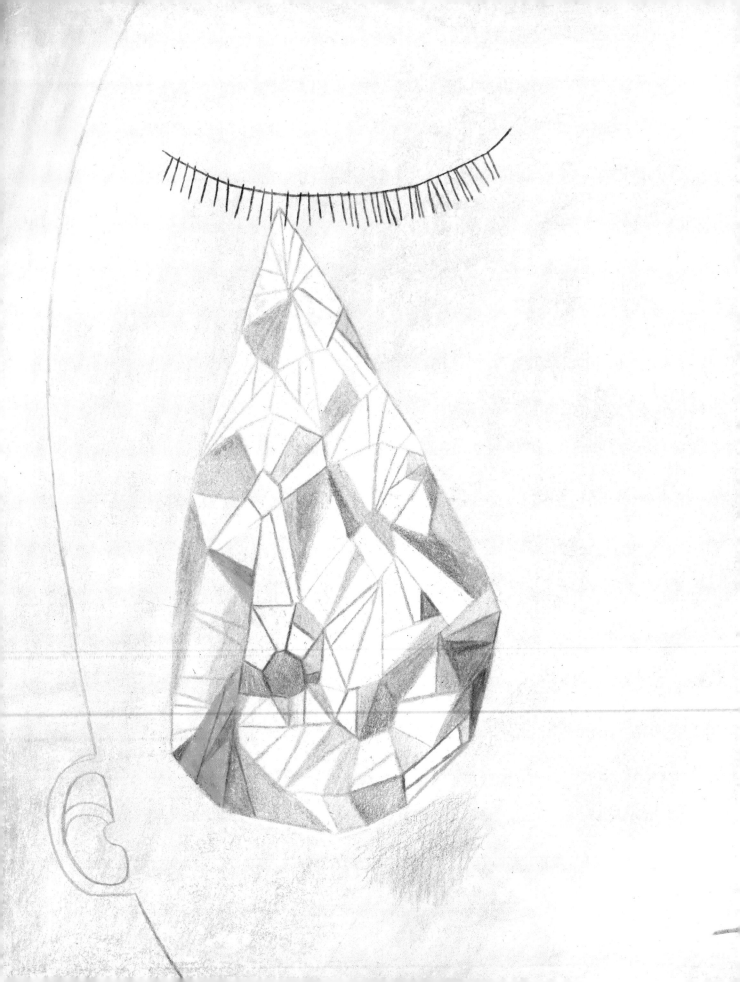

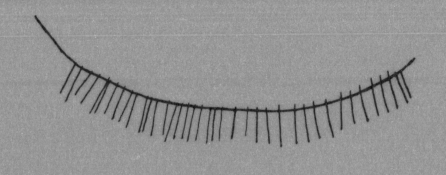

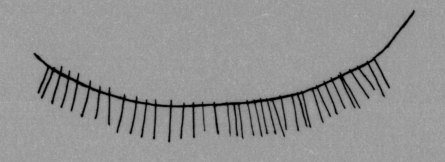

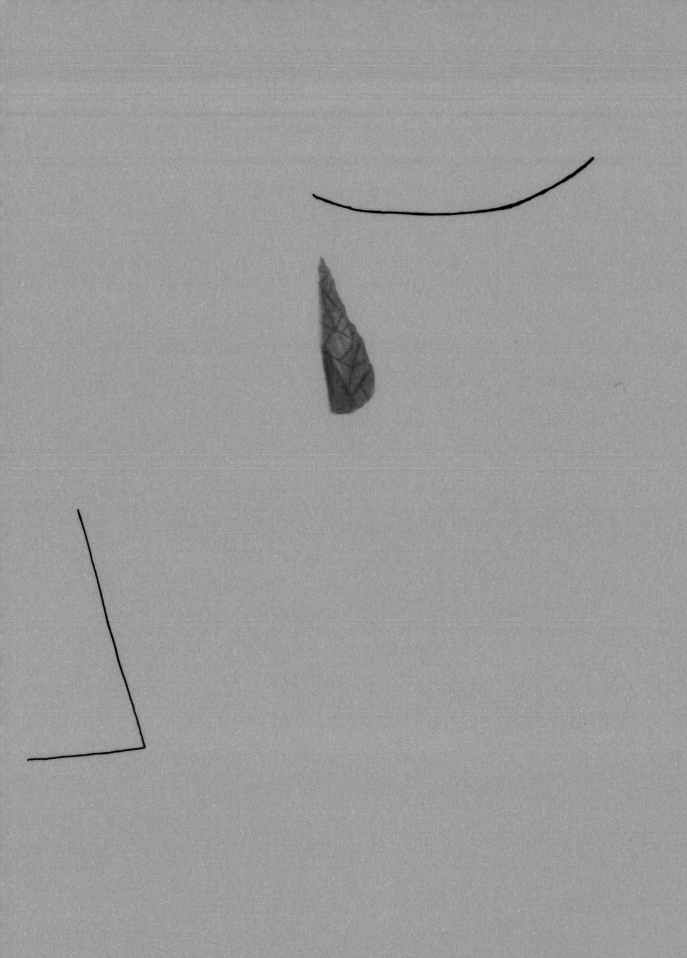

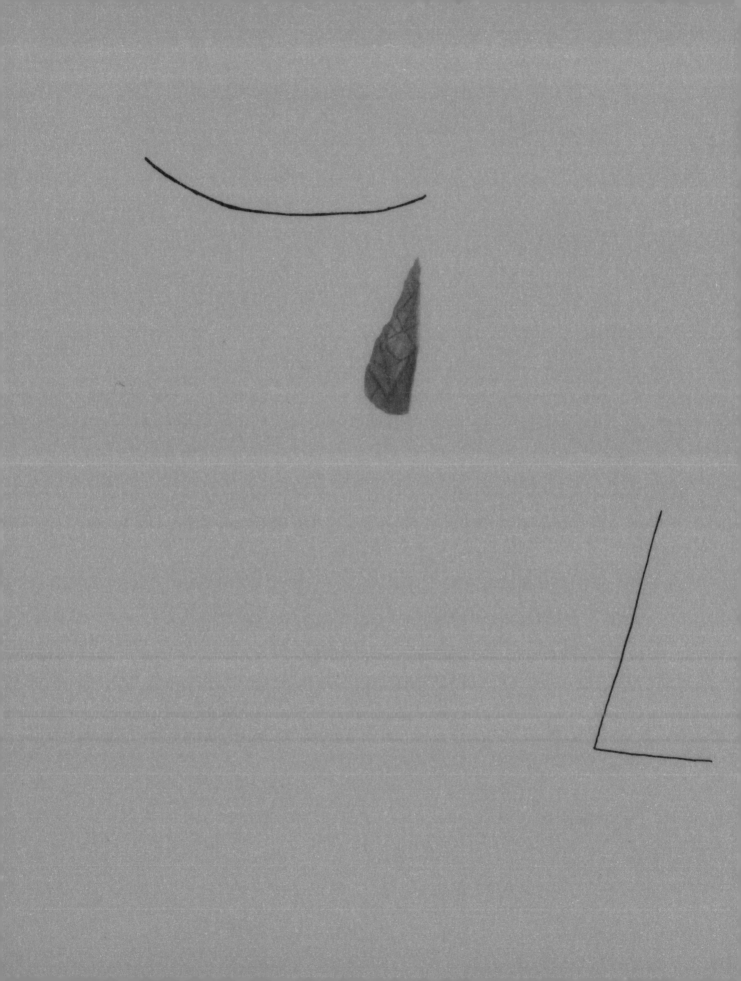

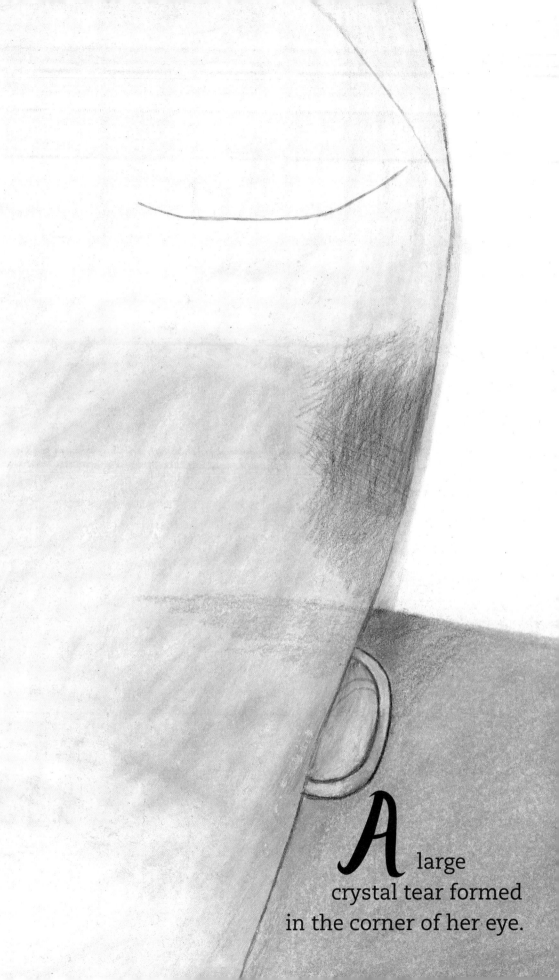

A large
crystal tear formed
in the corner of her eye.

But everywhere she went, it was the same. Everyone avoided her. And so, after a few days, she would repack her bags and leave again. She went from city to city, country to country. Wherever she went, she was rejected.

Until the day when she had had enough of leaving and looking for the place where she might fit in.

On that day, content within herself, she turned around and went home. Even though the truth could be scary and people preferred to ignore it.

Once home, Gisele lived
her life as she was.

Sparkling and luminous,
sensitive and transparent,
but resolute.

Completely whole in herself,
at last.

The End